Alan Schroeder / Illustrated by Yoriko Ito
Lily and the Wooden Bowl
A DOUBLEDAY BOOK FOR YOUNG READERS

A Doubleday Book for Young Readers
Published by Delacorte Press
Bantam Doubleday Dell Publishing Group, Inc.
1540 Broadway
New York, New York 10036

Doubleday and the portrayal of an anchor with a dolphin
are trademarks of Bantam Doubleday Dell Publishing
Group, Inc.
Text copyright © 1994 by Alan Schroeder
Illustrations copyright © 1994 by Yoriko Ito

Library of Congress Cataloging in Publication Data
Schroeder, Alan.
Lily and the wooden bowl : a Japanese folktale / adapted
by Alan Schroeder ; illustrated by Yoriko Ito.
p.   cm.
Summary: A young girl who wears a wooden bowl over
her face to hide her beauty overcomes a variety of trials
and eventually finds love, riches, and happiness.
ISBN 0-385-30792-6
[1. Fairy tales.   2. Folklore—Japan.]   I. Ito, Yoriko,
ill.   II. Title.
PZ8.S3125Li   1994   398.2—dc20
93-17900   [E]   CIP   AC

Typography by Lynn Braswell
Manufactured in Italy
October 1994
10 9 8 7 6 5 4 3 2 1

Author's Note

In adapting this Japanese folktale, certain changes have been made. In traditional versions of the story, none of the characters are named; there is no paper crane or wooden rice paddle; and at the beginning of the tale, Lily lives with her parents, not her grandmother. Nor, after falling in love, is Lily forced to pass any test imposed upon her by her future mother-in-law.

One version of this story, "The Wooden Bowl," can be found in *Japanese Fairy Tales* by Lafcadio Hearn and Others (Boni and Liveright, 1918). A recent retelling appears in Eric Quayle's *The Shining Princess and Other Japanese Legends* (Arcade Publishing, 1989).

To Richard
and Karen Babineaux,
with love.
—A.S.

To Hiroshi O.
for hearing the sound
of motorcycles.
—Y.I.

Long ago, when Japan was still known as "The Island of the Dragonfly," there lived an old woman named Aya and her young granddaughter Lily. Lily was a beautiful girl: her eyes were as brown as the rich summer soil, her lips were as pink as the budding azalea blossoms, and her skin—her skin was as fair as the snows that dusted the distant peaks of Mount Fuji.

Like many people in their province, Lily and her grandmother were extremely poor. When Aya finally lay upon her deathbed, she had but two things to pass on to her grandchild: a small wooden rice paddle and a folded paper crane.

"Take these things," she said to Lily. "If all goes well, they may bring you great luck someday."

The sun was beginning to set, and Lily wanted to fetch the herbalist, but the old woman begged her not to leave.

"In a few hours," Aya said gently, "I shall be passing across the Floating Bridge of Heaven. Before I go, there is one thing I must do." With a wrinkled finger, she touched her granddaughter's snowy cheek. "Your face, child, will tempt many men. I fear they will spoil your innocence and I cannot let that happen. Therefore we must hide your beauty from the world."

She reached for a large lacquered bowl, and turning it upside down, she placed it upon her granddaughter's head. The wooden bowl came all the way down to Lily's nose, completely hiding the upper part of her face. It was a peculiar sight, but Aya seemed satisfied. Taking Lily's hand, she made the girl promise that she would never remove the wooden bowl from her head. "Like the other things I have given you, it will protect you and watch over you after I am gone."

When Aya died, Lily was left alone in the world. To earn her living, she became a worker in the neighboring rice fields. All day long she stood in one position, her back bent, fingers moving, the wooden bowl shading her eyes against the sun. At the end of each day, Lily's hands were cracked and bleeding.

The other workers continually teased and tormented her, trying to knock the bowl into the mud. One day, however, an amazing thing happened. The folded paper crane, which Lily always kept nearby in an open basket, was suddenly swept up by a sharp gust of wind. Curving and diving in the air, it beat its wings, chasing away anyone who came too near.

"Awk! Awk!" it cried in a tight, angry voice.

The other workers were terrified, and in this strange but loving way the paper crane protected Lily, just as her grandmother had promised it would.

A few days later, Lily was approached by Yamoto, the wealthy farmer who owned the fields. She noticed at once the worried look on Yamoto's face.

"My wife, Matsu, is ill," he explained, "and I need someone to nurse her back to health."

Lily must have hesitated, for Yamoto quickly added, "Matsu and I will treat you with great kindness. Indeed, we will treat you as if you were our own daughter."

It was a generous offer, and Lily gratefully accepted.

Yamoto's house, she discovered, was large and very grand, with mirrors and hanging scrolls and beautiful woven mats in every room. Yet despite this luxury, Lily was not happy. Yamoto's wife was a cruel and spiteful woman, with eyes as black as pitch and a smile as cold as the River of Death. Matsu despised Lily from the moment she laid eyes upon her.

"Who is this girl," she demanded, "and why does she wear that ugly bowl upon her head? How dare she draw attention to herself in my household!" And from that moment forward, Matsu swore that she would not rest until she had driven the girl from the house in disgrace.

It was about this time that Yamoto's eldest son returned from the city of Kyoto, where he had finished his studies. His name was Kumaso, and he was a good-hearted, handsome young man, with eyes as merry and lively as two kites dancing in the summer wind.

One day, Kumaso startled his mother by asking, "Who is the new servant girl? And why does she wear that wooden bowl upon her head?"

Matsu eyed her son suspiciously. "It is a very sad story," she said. "The girl's name is Lily. As a child, she suffered from smallpox. Her face is badly scarred, and that is the reason she wears the bowl upon her head. Keep away from her, son. She is slow and dim-witted and will soon be returning to the rice fields, where she belongs. Do not give her another thought."

But Kumaso was unable to heed his mother's words. In the weeks that followed, he found himself watching Lily, admiring the quiet, graceful way she went about her chores. His curiosity soon turned to love, and he began to meet Lily whenever she came out to fetch water from the well.

Kumaso's manner was gentle and lighthearted, and by the time the snow had melted, Lily had fallen deeply in love with him. Their happiness, though, was frustrated by one thing: Kumaso could not convince Lily to remove the wooden bowl from her head.

"If we are to be married, I must see your face," he told her, but Lily refused. As much as it hurt her, she could not break the promise she had given her grandmother.

Kumaso, however, was impatient. One day, without warning, he lifted his hand to remove the bowl himself. At once, the paper crane rushed from Lily's basket. As it beat its wings furiously, Lily fled from the courtyard, tears streaming down her cheeks.

Kumaso could have followed, but his feet remained fixed to the ground. For one instant, he had caught a glimpse under the bowl, and the sight of Lily's face had taken his breath away. Her eyes were like moist jewels swimming in darkness, and her cheeks—her cheeks were as pure and as white as the finest porcelain. Never before had Kumaso seen such beauty. That very evening he went to his parents and told them that he had made his choice: he would have no woman but Lily for his wife.

With a glad heart, Yamoto welcomed the idea of becoming Lily's father-in-law. Matsu, however, was greatly angered. Pushing Yamoto aside, she gripped her son by the wrist.

"There will be no marriage," she said sternly. "Can't you see that the bowl is a trick? Naturally, Lily wishes you to think she is beautiful. In fact, just the opposite is true. I have seen her face myself—it is painful to the eye."

But Kumaso was not easily discouraged. He loved Lily, and he was determined to marry her. As he told his father, it would be easier for him to change the direction of the wind than to disobey his heart.

Matsu, however, was a cunning woman who would do anything to get her way. One night,

after much quarreling, she pretended to give in to her son's wishes.

"As you know, I do not approve of this marriage," she told him. "I will, however, give my consent...on one condition: I want Lily to prepare the rice for your wedding feast."

Kumaso was about to speak, but Matsu raised her hand.

"Keep silent until I am finished. If Lily succeeds in cooking enough rice for one hundred people, I will give my blessing and the wedding will take place tomorrow. If she fails, she leaves the house at dawn and all talk of marriage between you will cease."

Kumaso did not realize how treacherous his mother could be. Without thinking twice, he agreed to the unusual test.

Matsu wasted no time in finding Lily. Taking her by the arm, she dragged the girl to the dimly lit kitchen.

"You have not fooled my son entirely," she said. "Before there is to be any wedding, he demands that you prove your worth by carrying out one simple task."

Matsu took from her pocket a single grain of rice, which she dropped into a large, deep cooking pot. "You have until dawn to prepare enough rice for one hundred people. If you fail, there will be no wedding...ever."

Before Lily could say a word, Matsu withdrew from the kitchen, locking the heavy door behind her.

Lily's eyes filled with tears. How was it possible to prepare a potful of rice from just one tiny grain? Then, as if in a dream, she heard her grandmother's voice. "Take this rice paddle," Aya said lovingly. "It may bring you great luck someday."

Lily reached deep into her pocket and brought out the long-forgotten paddle. She could not imagine what good it would do. Nevertheless, she poured a tiny bit of water into the cooking pot and began to stir it. At first, nothing happened. Then, to her amazement, the rice began to separate into two, three, four, five grains. Ten grains became twenty, twenty forty, and so on, until the iron pot was filled to the brim. Lily could hardly believe her wonderful luck.

At that moment, Matsu peered through a crack in the wall. When she saw the mountain of rice, she knew she had been tricked. But Matsu had a trick of her own, one she had learned from an old sorceress in Kyoto. By ringing a tiny bronze bell over a burning candle, she was able to summon every hungry rat from the surrounding fields and marshes. And because she had learned well from the sorceress, Matsu spoke to the rats and told them in their own language exactly what it was she wanted them to do.

Lily, meanwhile, was setting out the rice for the wedding guests. She was reaching for the last bowl when, suddenly, dozens of squealing rats began pouring into the kitchen. Petrified, Lily watched as the rats attacked the rice, flipping over the bowls, burrowing their noses into the steaming white mounds. It was a horrible sight: tails and whiskers and broken crockery everywhere. The starving rats ate till their bellies sagged to the ground. Then, satisfied, they scurried out again through the cracks and crevices, leaving Lily crouching in the shadows, shaking with fear.

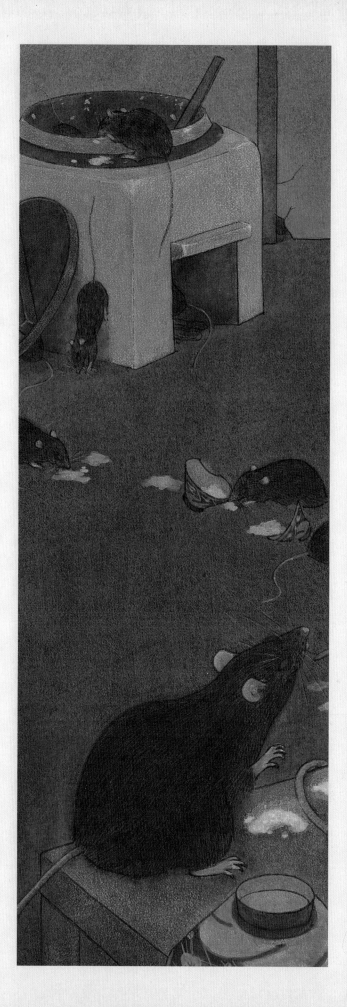

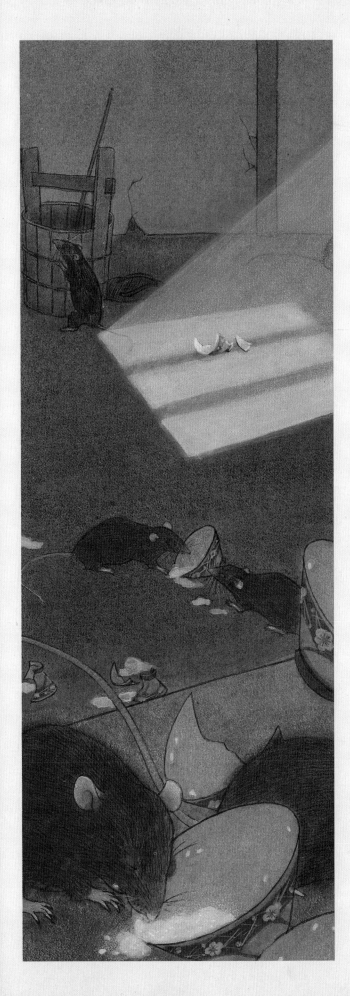

A few minutes later, a key turned in the lock and Matsu entered the kitchen. Without even glancing at Lily, she strode to the cooking pot and peered in. A smile came to her lips, for there, resting at the very bottom, was the same grain of rice Lily had started with.

"I knew you would fail," Matsu said with a smirk. "Now go. Go, before my son sees you." When Lily did not move, Matsu seized a heavy bamboo stick. "Go, I said! Leave this house immediately!"

Her shouting could be heard in every room, and father and son came running. Yamoto stopped short in the doorway, horrified by what he saw: his wife, with the bamboo stick raised above her head, and Lily, crouching, ready to receive the blows.

"What is going on here?" he demanded, snatching the stick from Matsu's grasp. Tearfully, Lily told Yamoto all that had happened. The farmer could not believe what he was hearing.

Matsu glared at Lily. "Obviously, the girl is lying," she told her husband boldly. "Look about you: Do you see a single rat anywhere in this kitchen? The stupid girl broke the rice bowls herself. Send her away, I tell you!" By now, Matsu had worked herself into a fit. She pointed angrily at Lily. "Either she goes, or I go!"

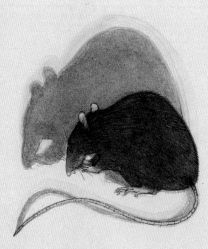

It was a painful decision for Yamoto, but in his heart he knew that Lily was telling the truth. Taking the girl's hand, he joined it with that of his son. "Rice or no rice," he told them, "the wedding will be held this very afternoon, under the cherry blossoms in the garden." Then, turning to Matsu, he said sternly, "You have shown yourself to be dishonest and cruel, and therefore unworthy of the family name. Take your possessions and go. I do not wish to see you again."

And so it happened that Matsu was sent away from the province in disgrace, never to be heard from again.

The wedding was held that very afternoon, just as Yamoto had promised. One hundred guests attended the ceremony, and Lily's bountiful paddle provided all the rice anyone could wish for.

When the bride appeared in her white kimono, everyone felt that it was time for Lily to remove the wooden bowl from her head. Lily knew she could not delay this moment any longer. But when she tried to take off the bowl, it would not budge. Yamoto and several relatives tried to help. They tugged and pulled, but the bowl uttered such frightful groans that they immediately backed away.

The elders advised that the wedding should be called off. But Kumaso was determined to marry Lily. Taking her by the hand, he said gently, "Do not worry. With or without the bowl, you will always be dear to me." Then he made a simple gesture, indicating that the ceremony should proceed. Now came the moment for the bride and groom to drink the "three times three," to show they had become husband and wife.

As Lily brought the wine cup to her lips, the wooden bowl gave a violent shudder. Splitting in half, it released a tremendous shower of emeralds, sapphires, and diamonds; gold, pearls, and jade; fabulous star rubies from faraway Ceylon—all these riches, and more, fell to the ground in a sparkling pile.

But the most astonishing treasure of all was the beauty of the bride, revealed for the first time to the eyes of the world.